To Shiv and Veer

For making me 'Amma'

Vakratundh Mahakaya Suryakoti Samaprabha

Nirvighnam Kuru Me Deva Sarva Karyeshu Sarvada

O Lord, of the curved trunk and immense body,

Radiant with the brilliance of the sun,

Pray clear all obstacles from

All of my endeavors forever.

The drum beats grew louder,
People danced in a frenzy.
The chanting grew intense
As they got closer to the sea.

Surrounded by hundreds of people
Were huge idols - ten, twenty feet tall,
Of the elephant God, Ganesha,
Towering above them all!

Chants of "Ganapati Bappa Morya
Agle varas tu jaldi aa," filled every ear.
"O dear Ganesha," they sang,
"Hasten back to us again next year."

They were celebrating
Lord Ganesha's birthday,
A festival called Ganesh Chaturthi
Which falls on the new moon's fourth day.

Beautiful statues of Ganesha
Are carried to the sea with fanfare,
Placed on the rolling waves,
With ardent prayer and gentle care.

So we bid farewell to Ganesha,
And ask for his everlasting favour,
Praying for his return the next year
To bless us in our every endeavour.

After the day's festivities ended,
As Amma put Klaka and Kiki to bed,
They asked, "Amma, tell us about Ganesha
And how he got an elephant's head!"

Amma said, "Ganesha is the son of
Shiva and his wife Parvati.
The story of his elephant's head
Is rather long - so listen carefully.

They lived in the Himalayas,
A beautiful snow-capped mountain chain.
On a high peak called Mount Kailash,
Surrounded by a rocky terrain.

Shiva was a brilliant shade of blue,
Wore a tiger skin and a snake around his neck.
Long matted hair, a crescent moon on his brow –
You could say he was a maverick!

He often disappeared in the wilderness
For days on end, all by himself,
To meditate and get away from it all.
Parvati was often alone, fending for herself.

One day, she felt terribly lonely.

And told the mountains about her lack:

"I wish I had someone to play with."

"To play with, to play with," they echoed back.

Suddenly, Parvati had an idea!

"I will make a figure out of clay," she said.

She took sandalwood paste and moulded it

With arms, legs, a belly and a head!

The figure looked quite life-like!

"O, how I wish you were my child.

Perhaps I will make you come alive!"

Parvati exclaimed, and smiled.

So she blew life into the figure,
And a grand miracle took place!
A boy with big eyes and dimpled cheeks
Stood before Parvati - face to face!

"Amma, you're not alone anymore," he said.
"My son!" Parvati cried, with tears of joy.
She could not believe her wonderful luck -
She finally had her own little boy!

The next morning while Shiva was still away
As Parvati was going for a bath,
She told the boy to guard the entrance
"Let no one in, make sure you block their path."

The little boy was proud and pleased,
Ready to be a guard for his mother.
He'd take on all who tried to enter
Be it a friend, a father or brother.

And it so happened that Shiva
Returned to his home that very day.
He found the young lad at his front door,
Standing there firmly and blocking his way.

"Stop!" commanded the little boy.
"No one enters till my mother says so."
Shiva laughed, "Do you know who I am?
Child, this is my home, let me go."

"I don't care who you are!
I'm carrying out my mother's wish, go away!"
Shiva was irritated and said,
"Little brat, this is not child's play."

It was beneath Shiva's dignity
To, fight a mere boy. So he sent
His pet bull Nandi and his followers, 'ganas'-
And to confront the boy they went.

But the ganas were no match
For this fearless little fighter.
The boy defeated them all
Though he was smaller and lighter!

An angry Shiva sent Bramha to tame the boy,
And as soon as Bramha appeared,
The boy played a prank, jumping on him
Pulling hard at his moustache and beard!

"Aah!" Bramha shrieked in pain,
And holding his injured face,
He ran away to tell Shiva
Of his embarrassing disgrace.

Now, Shiva had had enough!
"I am ready for a face-off," he said.
He threw his trident blade in the air.
It found its aim and off flew the boy's head.

When Parvati arrived at the scene,
She was horrified to see
The boy she had created and loved
Lying dead, his head severed dreadfully.

Her cries shook heaven and earth,
For a mother's grief is a powerful force.
Nothing could make her feel better.
Parvati cried till she was hoarse.

From her forehead sprang the Goddess Kali
And together they vowed to avenge the child.
They rampaged the earth like a whirlwind,
Destroying everything with anger so wild.

A desperate Shiva pleaded with her.
"Parvati, please stop, I beg you!
Heaven and earth will be ripped apart
If thus you and Kali continue."

She glared at Shiva with blazing eyes.
"You killed my son, this is all your fault!
If you want to preserve this earth
Then undo your sin and my rage will halt."

Shiva understood and said,
"I'm sorry. I didn't know he was our son.
I will search for his head, far and near.
I won't rest till this calamity is undone."

Shiva set off to find the boy's head,
But the blow had sent it far away.
He searched and searched with no success,
And finally sat down in dismay.

A nearby elephant saw Shiva,
And asked, "Why do you look so sad?"
Shiva said, "I beheaded an innocent child.
In anger, I did something very bad."

The elephant said, "I am old,
And my life will soon finish.
Please take my head for the child
So you can end your anguish."

Shiva had tears in his eyes.
He said, "O wise one, I thank you.
Without you, I would not have known
What I could possibly do."

With the elephant's head in his arms,
Shiva ran home with no time to spare.
He put the head on the child's body
And Parvati gently stroked his hair.

Slowly the boy opened his eyes!
Parvati hugged him, saying "My little one!"
Shiva said, "Forgive me for my foolishness.
I love you, for you are also my son."

"Since you were so brave a guard,"
Shiva said, "Now I shall proclaim,
You will be the leader of my ganas
And Ganesha shall be your name."